Who's Afraid of Fourth Grade?

For Bonnie B.
A super special friend and editor—N.K.

To Rauni and John,
with love—J&W

If you purchased this book without a cover, you should be aware that this book is stolen property. It was reported as "unsold and destroyed" to the publisher, and neither the author nor the publisher has received any payment for this "stripped book."

The scanning, uploading, and distribution of this book via the Internet or via any other means without the permission of the publisher is illegal and punishable by law. Please purchase only authorized electronic editions, and do not participate in or encourage electronic piracy of copyrighted materials. Your support of the author's rights is appreciated.

Text copyright © 2004 by Nancy Krulik. Illustrations copyright © 2004 by John and Wendy. All rights reserved. Published by Grosset & Dunlap, a division of Penguin Young Readers Group, 345 Hudson Street, New York, New York 10014. GROSSET & DUNLAP is a trademark of Penguin Group (USA) Inc. Printed in the U.S.A.

Library of Congress Cataloging-in-Publication Data

Krulik, Nancy E.
  Who's afraid of fourth grade? / by Nancy Krulik ; illustrated by John & Wendy.
     p. cm. — (Katie Kazoo, switcheroo)
  "Super special!"—Cover.
  Summary: As long-awaited fourth grade starts, Katie is overwhelmed when the magic wind causes her to switch twice—first into a new classmate and then into Mr. Starkey, the school band leader.
  ISBN 0-448-43555-1 (pbk.)
  [1. Schools—Fiction. 2. Bands (Music)—Fiction. 3. Magic—Fiction.] I. Title: Who is afraid of fourth grade?. II. John & Wendy. III. Title.

PZ7.K9416Who 2004
[Fic]—dc22

                    2004000414

     ISBN 978-0-448-43555-8   20 19 18 17 16 15 14

KATIE KAZOO, SWITCHEROO

Who's Afraid of Fourth Grade?

by Nancy Krulik • illustrated by John & Wendy

Grosset & Dunlap

ROWLETT PUBLIC LIBRARY
WITHDRAWN
ROWLETT, TX 75088

Chapter 1

"Hurry up, Katie," Suzanne Lock urged her best friend, Katie Carew. "I'm just *dying* to find out what teacher I've got this year!"

Every year, Katie and Suzanne made this same trip on the day before school began. Even though Cherrydale Elementary School was closed, the class lists were posted on the front doors. All the kids in town came to the school to find out who their teachers would be—and which of their friends would be in their classes.

Katie picked up her speed. She was excited to find out who her fourth-grade teacher was going to be too.

"Girls, wait up!" Katie's mother shouted, following close behind them.

As she raced toward the school building, Katie thought back on how she'd felt this time last year. She remembered how upset she and Suzanne had been when they'd found their names listed under class 3A. That was Mrs. Derkman's class. Mrs. Derkman was the strictest teacher in the whole school!

But they had survived Mrs. Derkman *and* third grade. Now they were going to be in fourth grade. The *Upper* Elementary School!

Katie knew that fourth grade would be full of changes. In fourth grade, you got real textbooks to keep for the whole year—not just worksheets that the teachers handed out. The fourth, fifth, and sixth-graders all got to play in the big yard—the one *without* the swings and seesaws. Plus, the Upper School's yard had a real baseball diamond and a soccer field.

But the most exciting thing of all to Katie

was that this year, she could sign up to play an instrument in the beginning band! Katie wanted to learn to play the clarinet, just like her mom had.

No doubt about it. Fourth grade was going to be awesome!

"I sure hope I get Ms. Sweet," Suzanne huffed as she ran. "She's gorgeous! She wears the coolest clothes and really funky high heels. Not dorky, old dresses and flat shoes like Mrs. Derkman."

"She's supposed to be really nice," Katie added. "That's even more important than what she wears."

"Whatever," Suzanne muttered as she reached the front door of the school.

A crowd of kids was gathered around the door, searching the lists for their names. Suzanne grabbed Katie's arm and elbowed a few smaller kids out of the way so she could reach the front of the crowd. "Okay, let me see."

"Hey, move over," Katie stood behind Suzanne and tried to see over her friend's shoulder. "I want to see too."

"There I am!" Suzanne squealed excitedly.

She placed her finger under her name. "Class 4B, *Ms. Sweet*. Oh, yeah!"

"Is my name there?" Katie asked, still not able to see the list.

"Zoe Canter's in my class," Suzanne continued, without answering Katie's question. "Miriam Chan and Manny Gonzalez too. We've got Jessica Haynes, and that computer whiz, Sam McDonough. Becky Stern's here too. And *oh, no*."

"Oh, no what?" Katie asked her.

"Jeremy Fox. I can't believe I'm stuck with him again!"

Jeremy! He was Katie's other best friend. Now Katie *really* wanted to be in class 4B. "How about *me*?" she asked again.

Suzanne shook her head. "Sorry, Katie. You're in 4A."

Katie couldn't believe it. She pushed Suzanne out of the way and looked at the list. It was hard to see through all the tears that were forming in her eyes. Katie wiped her eyes. Yes, it was true. Her two best friends were in the same class, with the best teacher, and she wasn't with them! That was not fair!

"You've got the new teacher, Mr. Guthrie," Suzanne pointed out.

Katie didn't say anything.

"Don't feel so bad," Suzanne comforted her. "You've got some cool kids in your class too. Mandy Banks is with you, and both Emma Stavros and Emma Weber. Gosh, we haven't been in a class with Emma W. since kindergarten. And . . . uh-oh."

"What?" Katie demanded. "What's the problem?"

"Nothing except . . ."

"Except *what*?"

"Well," Suzanne said slowly. "George Brennan and Kadeem Carter are both in your class. You know how much trouble those two can be on their own. I can't imagine what they'll be like together!"

Katie groaned. George was a real joker. He

thought he was the funniest kid in the entire school. And he probably was—except maybe for Kadeem. He was pretty hilarious too. She had a feeling that George and Kadeem weren't going to get along too well.

"Come on, it won't be so bad," Suzanne said, trying to make Katie feel better. "You've got Kevin in your class, and he's not so bad—for a boy, anyhow. He'll probably be trying to break another tomato-eating record. Andy Epstein's in 4A too. He's a great soccer player. You guys might win a few games against us."

But that didn't make Katie any happier. "I don't know," she said. "You still have Jeremy. He's the best soccer player in the whole grade."

"Jeremy. *Ugh*. Don't remind me," Suzanne groaned.

"You and I will still see each other all the time," Suzanne continued. "At lunch, recess, and after school. And don't forget, you and Jeremy will still have your Wednesday afternoon playdates."

That was true. No matter what the other kids signed up for after school, she and Jeremy were always careful not to plan any activities on Wednesday afternoons. That was their special time to hang out.

"I do look forward to Wednesdays," Katie admitted.

"Wednesdays are going to be great for me too," Suzanne said. "That's the day I have my modeling classes."

"I know. You've told me about it a zillion times!" There was an angry tone in Katie's voice. She was kind of mad that Suzanne wasn't upset that they weren't in the same class.

"Mrs. Carew, can we go home now?" Suzanne asked, not even noticing how angry Katie had sounded. "I can't wait to call Zoe and tell her the good news!"

Chapter 2

"You need a dozen pencils," Mrs. Carew said when she and Katie were in the stationery store in the Cherrydale Mall later that afternoon. The school had mailed each student a school supplies list, so they could bring all their folders, notebooks, and pencils on the first day.

"Can I get the mechanical kind?" Katie pleaded. "I hate having to go to the sharpener all the time."

"Katie, they're so much more expensive than the regular ones," her mom reminded her. But she threw the pack of mechanical pencils into the basket, anyway. "You pick out two folders while I get your notebook paper in the next aisle."

Katie began sorting through the cardboard folders until she found just the ones she wanted. One had a brown and white cocker spaniel on the cover. She liked it because he looked a little like her dog, Pepper. The other folder she chose had a big unicorn surrounded by rainbows and silver stars.

Just then, Jeremy Fox and his mom turned the corner into the folder aisle. "Hi, Katie!" Jeremy called. "I saw the class list. I'm really bummed that we're not in the same class."

Katie smiled at Jeremy. At least *one* of her best friends was going to miss her in class this year. "It really stinks," she agreed.

"But we'll see each other," Jeremy promised her.

"I know," Katie replied. "So how was your week at sleepover soccer camp?"

"Awesome!" Jeremy told her. "I really improved. I just found out I made the

Cherrydale traveling soccer team!"

"Wow!" Katie congratulated him. Being on the traveling soccer team was a big deal. Only the best players in town got to be on that squad.

"I'm second string right now," Jeremy admitted. "But that's because I'm one of the youngest players. The coach said if I practice a lot, I could start a few games."

"Cool," Katie replied. "Maybe I could practice with you during our Wednesday playdates."

"Oh, I can't play with you on Wednesdays anymore," he said. "That's when the team practices."

"But we always . . ."

"It's not my fault," Jeremy interrupted her. "That's when the practices are. What can I say? Things change."

Katie sighed. As far as she was concerned, too many things were changing.

"Why don't you hang out with Suzanne on

Wednesdays?" Jeremy suggested.

"I can't. She's got modeling classes."

Jeremy shrugged.

"Can we pick another day?" Katie asked.

"I don't know. I'm really . . ."

"Katie!" Mrs. Carew called out, interrupting Jeremy.

"Gotta go," Katie said. She didn't want to hear the rest of Jeremy's answer.

"Ouch!" Katie cried. Her foot had gotten stuck in the bottom of one of the cardboard displays.

Bam! She tripped and fell. The display flipped over on top of her, and she fell to the floor. Hundreds of colorful cardboard folders showered onto her head.

Katie sat there in the middle of a huge pile of folders. Jeremy tried hard not to laugh. But he couldn't help it. She looked hilarious.

Katie glared up at her *supposed* best friend and scowled. "It's not funny!" she told him.

"It kind of is," Jeremy told her, biting his lip.

As Katie started to get up, Jeremy burst out laughing.

Katie looked over at Jeremy and rolled her eyes. "This day stinks!" Katie moaned.

Chapter 3

Katie was quiet all through dinner that night. She didn't feel much like talking.

"So, Katie, are you all packed for school tomorrow?" her father asked as they were eating dinner.

"I guess so."

"She's got a great new backpack," Katie's mom told her husband.

"I always loved the first day of school," Katie's dad recalled. "It was so exciting meeting my teacher, getting a nice clean desk, and seeing all my friends again."

"I won't be seeing my friends," Katie told him.

"That's not true," her mom reminded her. "They're still in your school. Plus, you've got some of your old friends in your class. You'll make new ones too."

"I don't want any new friends!" Katie exclaimed.

"Katie, that's just silly," Mrs. Carew replied. "Sometimes it's good to make new friends."

"What if Mr. Guthrie is mean? What if he's strict like Mrs. Derkman?"

Mr. Carew laughed. "Oh, I don't think anyone will ever be like Mrs. Derkman. She's one of a kind."

Katie frowned. "I don't want school to start. I wish . . ."

Katie was about to say she wished she'd never have to go to school, but she stopped herself. The trouble with wishes was, sometimes they came true. Katie knew all about what happened when they did.

It had all started one day at the beginning of third grade. Katie had lost the football game for her team, ruined her favorite pair of pants, and let out a big burp in front of the whole class. It was the worst day of Katie's life. That night, Katie had wished she could be anyone but herself.

There must have been a shooting star overhead when she made that wish, because the very next day the magic wind came.

The magic wind was a wild tornado that blew just around Katie. It was so powerful that every time it came, it turned her into somebody else! Katie never knew when the wind would arrive. But whenever it did, her whole world was turned upside down . . . switcheroo!

The first time the magic wind came, it had turned Katie into Speedy, class 3A's hamster! While Katie was Speedy, she had escaped from the hamster cage and wound up in the boys locker room—stuck inside George's stinky sneaker! Luckily, Katie had switched back into herself before George could step on her.

The magic wind came back again and again after that. Once, it turned her into Lucille, the lunch lady. Katie had started a food fight and almost got Lucille fired.

The wind had also changed Katie into other kids—like Jeremy, Becky, and Suzanne's baby sister, Heather. That time, things got really awful—Suzanne had tried to change her diaper! Good thing Katie had stopped her just in time.

Once, the magic wind turned Katie into her dog, Pepper. Cocker spaniel Katie had chased a really nasty squirrel into Mrs.

Derkman's yard—and had destroyed her teacher's favorite troll statue. Mrs. Derkman had definitely not been happy about that!

The switcheroos just kept on coming. Once, it turned her into Mrs. Derkman. Another time, it turned her into Genie the Meanie, her science camp counselor. That had been kind of scary—especially when Katie got all her friends lost in the woods overnight.

Then there was the time the magic wind changed Katie into Louie, the owner of the pizza place at the Cherrydale Mall. She'd spent an entire afternoon making pizzas for Louie's big pizza-eating contest. Katie was glad her mother hadn't known about that. Katie wasn't actually allowed to use an oven yet.

"I know one thing you can look forward to this school year," Mrs. Carew reminded Katie, interrupting her memories of the magic wind. "Your cooking lessons."

"Cooking lessons?" Mr. Carew asked.

"Katie found out that Jeremy had soccer practice on Wednesdays. That's when they usually have a playdate, and Katie was upset," Mrs. Carew explained. "So to cheer her up, I took her to Louie's for some pizza. Louie told us about a great cooking class for fourth-graders. They're giving it at the Community Center. We went right over and signed Katie up for Wednesday afternoon cooking classes."

Mr. Carew licked his lips hungrily. "Mmmm. I can't wait to taste all your new recipes," he told Katie. "Just think, maybe someday you'll make pizzas as well as Louie does."

Katie sighed. *If her father only knew.*

Chapter 4

By the time Katie arrived at the school yard the next morning, the classes were already lining up. She looked over at the line for class 4B. Suzanne was busy showing off her new jeans—black ones with silver zippers all over—to the other girls in class 4B. Miriam and Zoe seemed really impressed.

Katie usually hated it when Suzanne showed off. Sometimes, she even walked away when Suzanne began to brag. But today, Katie headed straight over to where Suzanne was standing.

"Nice pants," she complimented her best friend.

"Thanks," Suzanne replied. She looked at Katie's blue sweater, plaid skirt, and red high-tops. "Didn't you have those sneakers last year?" she asked Katie.

Katie shook her head. "These are new ones. They're a full size bigger."

Suzanne shrugged, unimpressed. "Hey, shouldn't you be standing with class 4A? They're over there." She pointed over to where the kids in *Katie's* class were gathered.

Katie couldn't believe how cold Suzanne was acting. Even though they were in different classes, she was still her best friend. Right? "See you after school," Katie muttered as she walked away.

As Katie got into line behind Emma W., her stomach started doing flip-flops. With Suzanne and Jeremy over there, and her over here, she was really afraid to start fourth grade.

"Hi, Katie," Emma W. said in her quiet, shy voice.

"Hi," Katie replied softly.

Emma studied Katie's face. "You wish you were in that class too, don't you?" she asked knowingly.

Katie nodded. "Jeremy, Suzanne, and I were always together . . . until now, anyway."

Emma sighed. "I know how you feel. Jessica and I have been in the same class since preschool. Now she's over there and I'm over here. It's going to be so weird."

Just then, George Brennan came charging up toward the line. "Hey, Katie Kazoo!" he greeted her.

Katie grinned—a little. She couldn't help it. She really loved it when George called her by the super-cool nickname he'd given her.

"Hi, George. Do you know Emma? She's in our class this year."

"Cool," George said, smiling at Emma.

"Did you have a good summer?" Katie asked.

"Yeah!" George exclaimed. "I went to this awesome beach resort that had a circus school for kids. I learned how to be a clown, and I got to try swinging on a trapeze."

"Wow!" Katie was impressed. "It sounds like fun."

"It was. I wanted to stay there forever. You know, run away with the circus."

"Sometimes I feel that way too," Katie agreed.

"Do you know what happened to the kid who ran away with the circus?" George asked her.

Katie shook her head. "What?"

"The police made him give it back!" George chuckled at his own joke. Katie and Emma giggled too. Nobody told jokes like George did.

Kadeem was standing just behind Katie and George. He didn't laugh at George's joke. Instead, he told one of his own. "What do you call a spoiled tightrope walker?" he asked Katie.

"What?"

"An acro-brat!" Kadeem laughed so hard, he almost fell down. "Get it?"

George frowned. "I get it," he said in a nasty voice. "And I wish I could give it back." He turned to Katie and Emma. "Now, do you want to hear a *real* joke? Why was the human cannonball fired?"

"Because he was acting like a big shot!" Kadeem finished George's joke for him. "That's an old one."

George's face turned really red. His eyes seemed to bulge out of his head.

Katie gulped. George was really mad. Suzanne had been right. Having George and Kadeem in the same class wasn't a good thing at all.

"Come on, George," Katie said, trying to steer him away from Kadeem. "Come inside with Emma and me."

"But that was *my* joke," George moaned. "He stole the punch line."

"It's okay," she whispered to him. "You

would have told it much funnier."

That seemed to make George feel better. He followed Katie and Emma into the school without saying another word.

"Oh, wow!" Mandy Banks exclaimed as she walked into class 4A.

"Check this out!" Emma S. agreed.

"This is the *coolest* room," Kevin Camilleri declared. He turned to Katie and George. "Nothing like Mrs. *Jerk*man's room, is it?"

Katie nodded. The room definitely wasn't anything like the neat, orderly room Mrs. Derkman had prepared for them when they'd arrived in third grade. The desks in class 3A had been arranged in even, straight rows. The walls had been almost bare, except for posters that said things like "Check Your Work" and "Learn to Ask Questions." Mrs. Derkman didn't like anything distracting in the classroom.

She definitely wouldn't have approved of class 4A. *This* classroom was totally wild! The bulletin board had been covered with neon-colored paper birds. Each of the kids' names had been written on a bird. Katie's name was on a yellow bird.

There were posters in the room too. But they didn't seem to have anything to do with school. The posters showed kids surfing, skateboarding, bike riding, skiing, and climbing mountains. A banner that read "Try Something New Today" was tacked up over the blackboard.

The classroom ceiling had been decorated with kites that were hanging from the light fixtures. The words "Fly to New Heights!" were written on some of them.

But the most amazing thing of all was that there were no rows of desks in the room. In fact, *there were no desks at all*. Instead, brightly colored beanbag chairs had been thrown into the middle of the room. The only regular chairs were beside a long table in the back of the room that was covered with mountains of twigs, yarn, glitter, tissue paper, pipe cleaners, and construction paper.

"What's this all about?" Katie whispered to Emma W.

"I've never seen a classroom like it," Emma whispered back. She fiddled nervously with one of her long, brown braids.

"Hey there, everybody." A deep man's voice filled the air.

Katie looked toward the blackboard in the front of the room. Or was it the back of the room? It was hard to tell, since there were no desks pointing in any direction.

Well, either way, Katie's new teacher was standing near the board. At least, she *thought* he was her teacher. The man didn't look like any teacher she'd ever seen before! He had long reddish-brown hair that he'd pulled back into a ponytail. He was wearing a pair of brown corduroy slacks, a jeans shirt, and a brown suede jacket.

"I'm Mr. Guthrie," he greeted them.

Okay, so he *was* her teacher.

"Put your backpacks over there by the coat hooks, then take a seat on one of the beanbags."

"*Any* beanbag?" Andrew asked, surprised.

"Sure. Pick a color you like," the teacher replied.

"Aren't you going to assign seats?" Kevin asked.

Mr. Guthrie shook his head. "Now why would I want to do that?"

Katie looked at her teacher's long hair and corduroy pants. She stared up at the kites on the ceiling. Then she studied the beanbags and the mounds of twigs, straw, and yarn in the back of the room. This didn't seem at all like school.

"Man, this year is going to be awesome!" George whispered to her.

But Katie wasn't so sure.

Chapter 5

"Okay, so I'll bet you're wondering why I've got all this junk here," Mr. Guthrie said. He walked over to the table that was covered with twigs, string, ribbons, and sticks. "Well, here's the sitch."

Katie looked at him strangely. "The *what*?" she whispered to Emma W. Emma was sitting in the pink beanbag right next to Katie's yellow one.

"He means the situation," Emma W. whispered back. "My big sister Lacey says that all the time."

"Our first science unit is birds," Mr. Guthrie explained. "And I think the best way to learn about birds is to *become* birds! So you're all going to spend the rest of the morning building your nests."

"Our *what*?" Andrew asked, surprised.

"Nests," Mr. Guthrie repeated. "Instead of desks and chairs, you're going to spend your days sitting in nests—at least until we've finished this unit." He smiled at all of their surprised faces. "First, let's put some paper on the floor, under your beanbags." He pointed to a big roll of brown paper.

"Then gather your materials from the back of the room. After you have your stuff, glue the twigs and sticks together in a big circle around your beanbag. After that, you can weave the yarn and ribbons into your nests."

"Is there any special way we should do it?" Mandy asked.

"Build it however you like. Your nest should reflect your personality. If you like soccer, you can glue a construction paper ball onto your nest. If you like flowers, make some

out of tissue paper and pipe cleaners. If music's your thing, you can decorate with musical notes and pictures of instruments. I want to be able to look at your nest, and know about you. It's a way we can get to know one another."

"So there are no rules?" Mandy asked, surprised. She was used to all the rules in Mrs. Derkman's classroom.

"Just one," Mr. Guthrie admitted.

Kadeem moaned. "I knew there would be a catch," he said softly.

"Make your nest sturdy enough to last a few weeks," Mr. Guthrie continued as if he hadn't heard Kadeem. "Just like a real bird's nest would be." He smiled broadly at the class. "Okay, little birds, go to work!"

George was the first one to jump out of his seat and start collecting twigs and yarn. Katie had never seen him so excited about an assignment before.

"You know what kind of bird Kadeem is?" George asked Kevin.

"What kind?"

"A chicken!" George laughed loudly. Kevin chuckled too.

Katie frowned. George was obviously still mad that Kadeem had ruined his joke this morning.

"In fact, he's a *crazy* chicken," George continued. "A cuckoo cluck!" He and Kevin laughed even harder.

Kadeem stopped what he was doing and stared at George. "At least I'm not the kind of bird you are. You're part chicken, part space alien. A real *eggs-traterrestrial*!"

Mr. Guthrie stared at the two boys.

"Uh-oh," Mandy whispered to Katie. "They're gonna get it now. You remember how mad Mrs. Derkman used to get when George told jokes during class?"

Katie nodded. It was hard to forget something like that.

But Mr. Guthrie didn't get angry at all. Instead, he started to laugh. "Hey, we've got comedians in this class. Rock on, dudes!"

Katie stared at her new teacher. *Rock on, dudes?* That wasn't the kind of thing a teacher said. At least not any of the teachers Katie had ever known. "You like jokes?" she asked, amazed.

"I love to laugh," Mr. Guthrie assured her. He turned to George and Kadeem. "Do you two dudes know the most important part of comedy?"

"Being funny?" Kadeem asked him.

Mr. Guthrie shook his head. "Nope. It's all about timing. And that's what you guys have to learn. There's a right time to kid around, but this isn't it."

"Sorry," George said quietly.

"I'll tell you what," Mr. Guthrie continued with a grin. "If you two can behave all day long, I'll let you have a joke-off at the end of the day."

"A joke-off?" George asked. "What's that?"

"It's kind of a contest," Mr. Guthrie told

him. "To see who can be the funniest dude in the class."

Kadeem rubbed his hands together excitedly. "I'm ready for that."

"Me too," George said.

"Cool," Mr. Guthrie told the boys. "Now let's get back to work. I want all you birds in your nests before lunchtime!"

Chapter 6

"Hey, Suzanne, wait up!" Katie shouted as she left school at the end of the day.

Suzanne was walking with Jessica Haynes, one of the girls in class 4B. They both stopped as Katie called out.

"Hi, Katie," Suzanne said. "How's Mr. Guthrie?"

"Kind of weird," Katie admitted. "But he's nice. But definitely not like any teacher we've had."

"Ms. Sweet is awesome!" Suzanne boasted. "She brought homemade cookies for us for snack. They were shaped like birds."

"And they were delicious," Jessica added.

"We had pretzel bites," Katie told her with a frown. She really didn't like pretzel bites.

"Bummer," Suzanne replied.

"But George and Kadeem had a joke-off at the end of the day," Katie added excitedly.

"A what?" Jessica asked, her hands on her hips.

"It's kind of a joke-telling contest. Mr. Guthrie lets them . . ."

"We drew pictures of our favorite birds," Suzanne interrupted. "I drew a peacock— with lots of gorgeous feathers."

Katie thought about telling her that she'd built a nest to sit in, but she changed her mind. Suzanne would probably just come up with something they did in her class that was even more wonderful. Or at least more *normal*.

"Oh. Well, anyway, I thought maybe you'd want to have a playdate," Katie said, changing the subject. "I have some homework, but we can . . ."

"Homework!" Suzanne was shocked. "On the first day? *We* don't have any."

Katie frowned. That didn't seem very fair.

"Anyway, Jessica and I already made plans for today," Suzanne continued.

"Oh, I just figured that since we didn't see each other all day, we could . . ."

Suzanne shook her head. "My mom thinks I should play with kids in my new class for a while, to get to know them better."

"Okay," Katie said quietly.

"Maybe in a few weeks, when we're used to being with other kids, we can play," Suzanne suggested.

"Sure. Whatever." Katie didn't know what else to say.

As Suzanne and Jessica walked away, Katie noticed that Emma W. was standing nearby. She seemed very sad.

"What's wrong?" Katie asked her.

"Jessica's *my* best friend," she explained quietly. "We play together all the time. But . . ."

She pointed toward Suzanne and Jessica, who were walking down the street arm in arm. A few tears began to form in Emma's huge brown eyes.

Katie knew just how Emma felt. "I know. Maybe *we* can do something together today," she suggested. "Do you want to come to my house?"

"Sure." Emma seemed happier. Then her face fell. "Except . . ."

"What's the problem?"

"It's just that today's my turn to take care of my little brother Matthew. He's in first grade. I was just going to pick him up in the school yard when I saw Jessica and Suzanne."

Katie smiled at her. "Why don't you bring Matthew too? Unless . . ."

"Unless what?"

"Well, is he afraid of dogs? Because I have a cocker spaniel and . . ."

"You have a dog?" Emma interrupted. "You're so *lucky*! I've always wanted a dog. All

I have are brothers and sisters."

"It's just me and Pepper," Katie said as the girls headed over to where the little kids lined up at the end of the day. "I can't believe Matthew's in first grade. He was just a baby when you and I were in kindergarten together."

Emma nodded. "He's not even the baby of my family anymore. The twins, Tyler and Timothy, are. They're two-and-a-half."

Wow! Katie was amazed. Emma had five kids in her family. That was a whole basketball team.

Katie was an only child. Lots of times, she had to play on her own or with Pepper. But her dog wasn't very good at board games. Katie bet Emma *never* had to be alone. She always had playmates around. Lucky Emma.

"There's Matthew," Emma said, pointing to a dark-haired boy in a pair of jeans with a tear in the knee. "Oh, boy. Those are brand-new jeans. Well, I guess I can sew a patch on them for him."

"You know how to sew?" Katie was amazed.

"Sure. My mom taught me," Emma said. "When you have so many kids, the big ones have to know things like that, so they can help out. Next I hope my mom's going to teach me to cook. That looks like more fun than sewing."

"I'm taking cooking classes on Wednesdays," Katie told Emma. "Maybe you can take them too."

Emma shook her head. "I'm not always free on Wednesdays. Sometimes I have to help out at home."

"Oh," Katie replied, a bit disappointed.

"At least I'm free today. You stay here. I'll go get Matthew. I can call my mom from your house and tell her what we're doing."

✕ ✕ ✕

Mrs. Carew was waiting on the front steps with Pepper when Katie, Emma, and Matthew got there. She had a big plate of cookies waiting beside her.

"Hi, Mom," Katie said, pulling her backpack

up the steps. "Do you remember Emma?"

"Sure," Mrs. Carew replied with a smile. "I haven't seen you in a long time."

"This is my brother Matthew," Emma told Katie's mom.

"Nice to meet you, Matthew." Mrs. Carew held out the plate of cookies. "Are you hungry?"

Matthew nodded. He took two cookies off of the plate and shoved them in his mouth.

"What do you say?" Emma coaxed him.

"Thank you," Matthew replied. Pieces of chewed-up cookie flew out of his mouth.

Emma bent down and scratched Pepper's chin. "Your dog is so cute," Emma told Katie. "I've always wanted a dog. But my mom says that taking care of five kids is enough work for her."

Mrs. Carew smiled. "I think your mother's right."

"So, do you want to do our homework first?" Emma asked Katie.

"You have homework?" Mrs. Carew asked.

"Can you believe it?" Katie answered. "On the first day!"

"Why don't we do our homework now?" Emma suggested. "It's so quiet here. It's never this peaceful at my house. Somebody's always running around or shouting about something."

"That sounds like fun!" Katie exclaimed.

"It is fun, *sometimes*," Emma agreed. "But it's also hard to get your work done that way. We could do our math homework really fast here."

"Pepper's already got a ball in his mouth," Katie pointed out. "How about we play now, and do our homework later? We have plenty of time."

Emma looked down at the happy cocker spaniel. He was hard to resist, especially for someone who wanted a dog of her own so badly. "Okay," she said finally.

Katie took the slobbery ball from Pepper's

mouth. She threw it clear across the lawn.

Katie and Emma laughed as both Matthew and Pepper took off after the ball.

"See, you have a dog too," Katie teased. "He's just got two legs and a pair of ripped pants!"

Chapter 7

The next morning, Katie walked into class 4A and placed her homework in the purple, black, and yellow box that sat on top of one of the cabinets. Then she went and perched herself in her nest.

Katie was really proud of her nest. She'd taken a lot of time making sure that the twigs and sticks were arranged in a neat circle around her beanbag. She'd brought in a picture of Pepper and glued it to her beanbag. Then she'd put black construction paper musical notes all around the sides to show that she was looking forward to being in the school band. Finally, she'd written "Katie

Kazoo" across the front of the beanbag with pieces of yellow yarn and glue so Mr. Guthrie would know her special nickname.

Katie picked up her plastic clipboard and began to copy down the vocabulary words on the board. Mr. Guthrie might not have any desks in his classroom, and he might say things like, "Rock on, dudes," a lot, but he was *still* a teacher. And, like any teacher, he expected the kids to start working the minute they walked into the classroom.

She looked up as Emma W. entered the room. Katie waved to her friend, but Emma didn't notice her. Instead, Emma walked nervously up to Mr. Guthrie.

"Hey, Emma, how's it going?" the teacher asked kindly.

"Not so great," Emma murmured. "I started to do my math homework last night. But when I got up to sharpen my pencil, my little brother used his safety scissors to cut up the paper." She looked shy and embarrassed.

Katie felt really bad. Emma had asked her if she could do the homework right when they had gotten to her house. But Katie had said no. She'd meant to do it later with Emma, but they had been so busy playing with Matthew and Pepper. Before they knew it, it had been time for Emma to go home. Katie had done her homework after dinner.

If she'd only said okay, this never would have happened to Emma. Now Mr. Guthrie was going to be mad.

But surprisingly, Mr. Guthrie didn't seem angry at all. In fact, he laughed. "Little brother, huh? I have one of those."

"I have *three*," Emma groaned. "And an older sister."

"Boy, you *do* have it rough!" Mr. Guthrie smiled kindly. "Just give it to me tomorrow. And, whatever you do, don't leave your homework alone," he teased. "You never know what kind of trouble a little brother can cause."

Emma smiled shyly as she took the homework sheet. "Tell me about it," she agreed.

The rest of the morning went quickly. Class 4A did their vocabulary, read the first chapter in their new reading book, and had a spelling bee. Other than his ponytail, and the fact that he made them sit in nests, Mr. Guthrie was a pretty normal teacher.

Around eleven o'clock, Mr. Guthrie announced that it was time for a mid-morning snack.

"Snack time is going to be part of our science lesson today," he told the class. "Now, some birds, like parrots, eat seeds and fruit. Other birds, like pelicans, eat fish. Does anyone know what kind of food a robin might eat?"

George's hand was the first to shoot up. "They eat earthworms and snails. They dig them up and munch them down." He made a loud slurping sound.

"Eew," Emma S. groaned. "Do you have to make it sound so gross?"

"Hey, I'm just telling it like it is," George replied.

"George is right," Mr. Guthrie agreed. "And today, *you* are going to be robins. If you want to eat your snack, you're going to have to dig for it."

"What's for snack?" Kevin asked.

"Oh, I thought I'd made that clear," Mr. Guthrie said as he walked over toward the small refrigerator in the corner. "You're all robins. So, of course, you'll be chomping on worms."

Katie gasped. Worms? For snack? Boy, had she been wrong about Mr. Guthrie. He wasn't a normal teacher at all. He was just plain creepy.

She watched as the teacher began to place small bowls of dark brown mud in front of each student. There were big clumps of dirt sitting in the mud. It was disgusting!

The kids just stared at their snacks. No one wanted to eat dirt and worms.

No one except *George*, that is. He leaned down and sniffed at his bowl of dirt. Then he grinned and happily shoved his face into the mud.

"Yum!" George sat up and smiled happily. His face was covered in mud. "It's chocolate pudding with chopped-up cookies in it."

"Chocolate!" Kevin exclaimed. He dug his face into the mud too. "Excellent!"

George buried his face in his pudding again. This time, he pulled out a worm! *Well, sort of.*

"Check it out! Gummy worms!" George opened his mouth and showed the class a half-eaten, orange-candy worm.

"That's gross, George," Mandy told him. She turned to Mr. Guthrie. "May I have a spoon, please?"

The teacher shook his head. "Sorry, Mandy. You're a robin, remember? Robins

don't eat with forks. They use their beaks to dig for worms."

"Like this!" Kadeem exclaimed. He buried his face in his bowl of mud and worms.

Soon all the kids were digging for worms.

"Yum! I found a blue-and-red one!" Andrew squealed happily. He held the gummy worm between his lips, and dangled it in front of Emma W.

Emma laughed, and began to dig through her own bowl of mud. "Here's a red-and-yellow one!"

"How about you, Katie Kazoo?" George asked her. "Aren't you going to dig for worms in the mud?"

Katie didn't answer him. Instead, she buried her face in her big, gooey mound of pudding and cookies. "Check it out, George!" she exclaimed, lifting her head from the mush. "I found half a green-and-yellow one."

"Where's the other half?" George asked her.

"I don't know. I'd better get back in there and look for it!" She buried her face in the mud again.

Yum! Maybe having a weird teacher like Mr. Guthrie wasn't so bad, after all. Chocolate and gummy worms for a snack! Katie figured that not even Ms. Sweet would do that! She had a feeling being in class 4A was going to be a lot of fun. At the very least, it wasn't going to be boring.

Who was afraid of fourth grade? Not Katie!

Chapter 8

Over the next few weeks, Mr. Guthrie taught the kids lots of fun stuff. One afternoon, he made them all stand on one foot and hide their heads under their arms—just to see how birds slept. Another day, he showed them how to do birdcalls, and the kids started a 4A birdcall chorus. Mr. Guthrie also took them on a field trip to a bird sanctuary, so they could see the animals in their natural habitat.

The kids in 4A were kind of cool too. Emma W. was really nice, and she liked dogs almost as much as Katie did! George and Kadeem kept everyone laughing with their joke-offs. And Kevin was still trying to break his tomato-eating record. He'd already eaten one hundred and thirty-five tomatoes—and it was just the beginning of the school year!

So far, fourth grade was great.

Except for Jeremy and Suzanne.

Katie understood why she didn't see Jeremy so much anymore. He was busy with soccer.

But Suzanne didn't have an excuse. Suzanne was acting like she didn't want to be Katie's friend at all. Katie talked to her mom about Suzanne. And her mom said that Suzanne had a point. It was good to try to make new friends. And she was sure that Suzanne was still her best friend. No matter what.

One day, Katie and Suzanne arrived at the playground at the same time on Friday morning.

"Hi!" Katie greeted her friend. "Aren't you glad it's Friday?"

"Nope," Suzanne said. "Friday's not my favorite day anymore."

"It's not?" Katie sounded surprised. "But the weekend starts right after school!"

"I know. But Wednesdays are my favorite days now. That's my modeling day."

"I love Wednesdays too," Katie agreed. "It's my cooking class day. Last week, we learned how to make cinnamon rolls from scratch. And we dipped strawberries in chocolate. You would have loved them."

"In modeling class, they told us to drink eight glasses of water a day," Suzanne said, changing the subject back to herself. "It's good for your skin. Next class, we're working on our hairstyles. The teacher is going to tell us what shape our faces are and . . ." Suzanne stopped suddenly. "Oh, there's Jessica," she said. "I have to tell her something really important. See you later, Katie."

Katie tried to remember what her mother had said about how it's okay to make new friends. But right now, she just felt like she wanted to cry.

Luckily, when Katie got into the classroom, Mr. Guthrie had some news that really cheered her up!

"It's time for beginning band sign-ups," the teacher announced. "I've got the forms right here."

Katie nearly burst out of her nest. "Oh, wow!" she exclaimed. "Can I have one right now?" Then she blushed. She was so excited, she'd forgotten to raise her hand.

But Mr. G. wasn't angry that she'd called out. In fact, he was happy to see her so excited. "That's the spirit! What instrument do you want to play?"

"The clarinet," Katie told him.

"Oh, the licorice stick," Mr. G. said.

"No, the clarinet."

Mr. G. smiled. "A lot of people call the clarinet a licorice stick because it looks a bit like licorice candy."

"I love licorice," George interrupted. "Especially strawberry-flavored; it's delicious."

"Then maybe you'd like to play the clarinet too," Mr. Guthrie suggested.

George shook his head. "Not me. I want to play the tuba." He stood up in his nest and pretended to wrap a giant tuba around his body. "Oompah, oompah," he said in a low, deep voice.

"I want the trombone," Kadeem added. "Whaa whaa, whaa whaa." He imitated a trombone's sound as he pretended to play one.

"I want to play the trumpet," Kevin piped in. "My big brother, Ian, can play Reveille on his. I want to be able to do that too." Kevin began singing the army's wake-up song.

Mr. Guthrie covered his ears. "Let's save the music for the school band director, Mr. Starkey," the teacher chuckled. "He's paid to listen to it! My job's just to hand out the forms."

That afternoon, Katie raced out of school, carrying her permission slip tightly in her hand. On her way out the door, she ran into Suzanne and Jessica.

"Hi," Katie greeted them. No matter what, she was going to be friendly toward Suzanne.

"Are you joining the band too?" Katie asked.

"Not me," Suzanne replied. "I'm going to be too busy modeling to practice an instrument."

"But your modeling class is after school on Wednesdays. That's just one afternoon," Katie reminded her. "I've got cooking then, and I'm still taking band."

"You never know what can happen. I might become a world-famous model and be traveling all the time. I couldn't be in the band then, could I?" Suzanne countered.

Katie knew better than to argue with Suzanne when she got like this. "How about you, Jessica?" she asked instead.

"Well, I was thinking about the flute,

but . . ." Jessica began.

"Jess is going to be my manager and personal assistant," Suzanne interrupted. "I'm going to need her with me all the time. There's no way she can fit band into a schedule like that."

Just then, the girls heard three loud, shrill whistles. Katie turned around and waved to Mandy, Emma W., and Emma S.

"What was that noise?" Suzanne asked her.

"Birdcalls," Katie told her. "Mr. G. taught them to us." She answered her classmates with a high-pitched trill of her own.

"That's bizarre," Suzanne told her. "In *our* class, we made bird mobiles from wire hangers and construction paper. We glued feathers to the birds."

"Sounds like fun," Katie admitted.

"It was," Suzanne told her. "*Everything* we do in our class is fun. That's why we're 4B."

"What are you talking about?" asked Katie.

Jessica laughed. "Don't you know? B stands for *better*. We're in the better class."

"No you're not," Katie argued. "Both classes are great."

"Katie, come on," Suzanne said. "You know you wish you were in our class. Just admit it."

"I don't wish anything!" Katie exclaimed.

Just then, Emma W. walked over to the group of girls. "Hi, Jessica. Hi, Suzanne," she said. Then she turned to Katie. "Are you still coming over today? We can practice birdcalls. Let's make up a bird song and do it for the class on Monday."

Suzanne and Jessica started to laugh.

"What's so funny?" Emma asked them.

"Oh, don't worry about them. They're just jealous because we're having so much fun in *our* class," Katie said finally.

"B is for better," Jessica and Suzanne began to chant. "4B is better."

Emma looked like she was about to cry.

Katie knew how she felt. Jessica used to be Emma's best friend. Now Jessica was being really mean. Just like Suzanne was being.

"Come on, Emma," Katie said, pulling her new pal by the hand. "We can't stand here talking to these birdbrains. We've got beautiful music to make."

Chapter 9

"Look at this place!" Katie exclaimed as she walked into Emma's house. She blushed. The words had left her mouth before she could stop them. But she couldn't help it. Emma's house was so different from Katie's. At Katie's house, everything was neat and orderly. The coats were always hung up in the closet, the magazines were stacked on the coffee table, and the dishes were put away.

But the Weber house was a mess! Baby socks were scattered on the floor of the front hall. There were toys everywhere. Katie had to be careful not to trip over a small truck or airplane as she followed Emma into the kitchen.

The mess came from having babies in the house. Katie remembered how clean and neat Suzanne's house had been—before her sister Heather was born. After that, there were bottles and toys all over the Lock house, too.

Suzanne! Just the thought of her made Katie angry. She decided not to think about her anymore. Instead, she followed Emma into the kitchen.

The kitchen wasn't any neater than the front hall. The sink was stacked high with unwashed baby bottles, and there were crumbs and part of an uneaten bagel on the floor just below the two high chairs.

Katie bet Mrs. Weber never made Emma clean her room the way Katie's mother always did. Emma sure was lucky! She could be messy if she wanted to.

But better than the mess was the fact that there were kids everywhere in the Weber house. By the time Katie, Emma, and Matthew got there, Emma's big sister, Lacey, was already home. The teenager was talking to one of her friends on the phone. Katie wasn't sure how Lacey could hear the person on the other end, since one of the twins was sitting on the floor, singing as he banged two pans together.

Katie stared at Lacey. The fifteen-year-old looked so cool. She had her long hair up in a messy bun. She was wearing glittery eye shadow and lipstick. Katie really loved her low-slung jeans and her silver belly shirt. Lacey's outfit was so much cooler than Emma's brown suede loafers and well-worn overalls. Katie thought how lucky Emma was that when she got older, she'd be able to share Lacey's awesome wardrobe.

Katie sighed. *She* didn't have anyone she could share clothes with.

Katie waited for Emma to introduce her to Lacey, but Lacey didn't even notice that the girls had entered the room. She didn't even notice that the twin who had been banging pots on the floor was now standing on the kitchen table.

"Tyler, get down from there," Emma said, setting the toddler on the ground.

"I'm firsty," he told her. "Want juice."

"Wouldn't Lacey get you a juice box?" Emma asked.

Tyler shook his head and pointed to Lacey. "Talk. Talk. Talk."

Emma sighed. "Lacey, get off the phone. It's your turn to help with the twins."

Lacey shot Emma a dirty look. She did *not* get off the phone.

Emma went to the refrigerator and took out a sippy cup filled with apple juice. "Where's Mom?" she asked Tyler.

Tyler pointed up toward the ceiling. "Timmy made stinky."

Katie looked confused.

Emma laughed. "He means Mom's upstairs changing Timmy's diaper," she explained.

Katie nodded. She smiled at Tyler. He

looked adorable drinking his juice, and rubbing a small baby blanket against his cheek.

Katie sighed. Emma was so lucky. She had cute little brothers, and a teenage sister too. Emma probably learned all about the latest styles and new music from Lacey.

"You want a snack?" Emma asked Katie.

"Sure. What do you have?"

Emma peeked in the cabinet. "We have graham crackers, peanut butter, and raisins. Mom usually leaves carrots and celery in the fridge too."

"Graham crackers sound good," Katie told her.

"Me too!" Tyler slid across the kitchen floor in his socks. He crashed into Katie's legs. "Oops, sorry."

Katie rubbed her knee. "It's okay," she assured him. She looked at Emma. "Is it always like this around here?"

Emma laughed. "You should see what's going to happen when Timmy gets down here.

He's the real troublemaker."

Just then, Katie heard a woman's voice shouting down the stairs. "Timmy, walk down the stairs like big boy. You shouldn't slide down on your tush."

"Bump. Bump. Bump," Timmy replied. He said "bump" every time he bounced down another step on his rear end.

Timmy and Mrs. Weber came into the kitchen. Timmy looked at his twin brother. He noticed that Tyler had his baby blanket. Timmy didn't have his. That did *not* make Timmy happy.

"WANT BLANKIE!" he cried out.

"Emma, will you go upstairs and get Timmy's blankie? I swear I can't go up those stairs another time." Mrs. Weber let out a weary sigh. "I'm so glad your dad's getting home from this business trip tomorrow night. I could sure use his help around here."

"I'll get the blankie, Mom," Emma replied sweetly. "Do you remember Katie?"

"Welcome to the zoo, Katie," Mrs. Weber joked. "I haven't seen you in so long. Why don't you go into the family room and make yourself at home while Emma runs upstairs? It's quieter in there." She pointed toward a room in the back of the house.

Katie looked at Emma.

"Go ahead. I'll be right back," Emma assured her.

As Katie left the room, she could see Mrs. Weber pull a package of chopped meat from the refrigerator. She was obviously starting dinner. Katie wondered how much food it would take to feed such a full house.

✕ ✕ ✕

The family room was quiet. Sure, there were plenty of toy cars, trucks, planes, and stuffed animals all over the place, but there was no one there. Katie sat down on the fluffy black couch and relaxed for a minute.

Now she knew why Emma wanted to do her math homework at the Carew house. Katie couldn't imagine how Emma got anything done with all the craziness going on in this house.

Still, things were kind of exciting at Emma's. There was no way anyone could ever be bored or lonely here!

Just then, Katie felt a cool draft on the back of her neck. She turned around and looked for an open window. But all the windows were shut tight. She looked up. There was no ceiling fan in the room.

The draft was getting colder and stronger by the second. But it only seemed to be blowing on Katie. There wasn't any sign of a breeze anywhere else in the room. Katie gulped. This was no ordinary wind.

This was the magic wind!

Whoosh! A powerful tornado began to swirl all around Katie. Faster and faster it spun, growing wilder by the second. Katie had to grab onto the couch to keep from being blown away. She shut her eyes tight, and tried not to cry.

And then it stopped. Just like that.

Katie gulped. The magic wind was gone.

Who had it turned her into this time?

Chapter 10

Slowly, Katie opened her eyes and looked around. She was still in Emma's family room. At least the wind hadn't blown her far away.

She glanced down at her feet. Her purple platform sneakers were gone. Now she was wearing a pair of brown suede loafers.

Katie's new jeans were gone too. Instead she was wearing a pair of faded overalls.

Slowly, she brought her hands up to her head. Her red curly hair was now brown. And it was bound into two thick braids.

Katie Carew was now Emma Weber!

"Oh, there you are, Emma," Mrs. Weber said, racing into the family room. She glanced around. "Where's Katie?"

How could she possibly explain *this*? "Um . . . she . . . um . . . I think she went to the bathroom or something," Katie mumbled quickly.

"Oh. Did you get Timmy his blankie?" Mrs. Weber continued.

"I . . . not yet . . . I mean, uh . . . I can go get it now," Katie said, although she wasn't at all sure where his blankie might be.

"Never mind. That's not important. Right now I have to go to the supermarket to get the rest of the food for dinner. Then I have to stop by the dry cleaners and the video store before they close. Can you bathe the twins for me while I'm gone?"

Katie had never bathed a baby before, never mind two. "But . . ." she stammered nervously.

"I know, it's Lacey's turn to take care of the twins," Mrs. Weber interrupted. "I just can't get her off that phone. So be a sweetheart and help me out, will you, Emma? I'm sure Katie won't mind. It'll only take a few minutes."

Mrs. Weber seemed so frazzled and tired. She really did need some help with the little kids. And it couldn't be any harder to bathe the twins than it was to bathe Pepper. Katie had done that plenty of times.

"Sure . . . *Mom*," Katie said finally.

Mrs. Weber bent down and kissed Katie on the cheek. "That's a good girl. I'll be home in an hour."

As Mrs. Weber left the house, Katie turned toward the kitchen. That's where she'd last seen the twins.

"Okay, Timmy and Tyler, it's bath time!" she announced, trying to sound very cheerful.

The boys weren't very happy about having a bath. In fact, they refused to go with Katie.

"No bath!" Tyler shouted, throwing his sippy cup.

"No bath!" Timmy echoed. He raced out of the kitchen.

"Come on, you guys," Katie urged. "It'll be fun."

Tyler shook his head hard. He ran into the hall, crawled into the front closet, and shut the door.

At least Katie knew where *he* was. She had no idea where Timmy had gotten to. "Timmy!" she called. "Timmy!"

But Timmy didn't answer.

Katie frowned. Where could that boy have gone?

She peeked into the downstairs bathroom. No Timmy.

She looked under the couch in the family room. No Timmy.

She opened the front closet. Maybe Timmy was hiding with his brother.

Tyler went racing out of the closet, running right past Katie. But Timmy was nowhere to be found.

Now Katie was getting worried. Had Timmy run out of the house? Was he outside and all alone? A little kid like him could get hurt out there.

This was *so* not good.

Chapter 11

"Aachoo!"

Suddenly, Katie heard a tiny sneeze coming from behind the drapes.

Yes! Katie moved the curtains to the side. Timmy had been hiding there all along. "There you are!"

"Aachoo." Timmy wiped his drippy nose on the drapes.

"Ooh, that's gross!" Katie exclaimed. "Let's go get a tissue. Then we'll have a nice, warm bath."

"No bath!" Timmy shouted. He zipped right past Katie into the kitchen.

Katie hurried after him. She was careful

not to trip over Matthew, who was sitting on the kitchen floor happily coloring with crayons. At least *one* of the Weber boys was being good!

But that didn't make up for Timmy and Tyler. At that very moment, Tyler was standing on a kitchen chair chanting, "No bath! No bath!"

Timmy scrambled up onto the chair next to his brother. "Hungry!" he declared. He reached out toward the kitchen counter.

Crash! Before Katie could stop him, Timmy knocked over a plastic container filled with tomato sauce. Mrs. Weber had accidentally left the sauce out before she'd gone to the supermarket.

A waterfall of tomato sauce splashed all over Matthew and his coloring book. "Oh, no! My picture!" Matthew cried out. "WAAAAHHHH!"

"Oops," Timmy said. He leaped from the chair and raced out of the room.

Tyler ran over to Matthew. He poked his chubby hand into a puddle of tomato sauce. "Yum!" he said as he licked his fingers.

"WAAAAHHHHH!" Matthew cried even louder. "Go away!"

Tyler did as he was told. He ran off toward the family room—leaving a path of tiny tomato sauce footprints behind him.

Finally, Lacey hung up the phone. "Can't you keep them quiet for five minutes? I couldn't hear a thing Beth was saying!" She looked around the kitchen and rolled her eyes. "Boy, Emma, I wouldn't want to be you when Mom gets home!"

At that moment, Katie didn't want to be Emma either. But she was stuck with it. And, as Emma, she was plenty mad at Lacey. "Hey, you were on the phone," she insisted. "You could have hung up and helped me!"

Lacey shook her head. "Don't blame this on me. Why did you say 'bath,' anyhow? You know they always run away when they hear 'bath.' "

But Katie *didn't* know that. She didn't know anything about the twins.

Lacey took Matthew by the hand. "Come on, Matty. We'll clean you up. Then you can color a new picture."

As Lacey and Matthew left the kitchen, Katie looked around. There was tomato sauce everywhere. It was obvious Mrs. Weber had been planning a meatballs and spaghetti dinner. Now there was no sauce.

Lacey was right. Dinner was ruined. Emma was in big trouble.

No. *Katie* was in big trouble. She was Emma. At least for now.

Suddenly, she felt kind of sorry for Emma. Katie had always wondered what it would be like to be part of a big family. Now she knew. While it could be fun to have lots of people around to play with, Emma never got to just be by herself. She probably would love a chance to get away from the other kids in her family. After all, her younger brothers weren't *always* cute. And having a big sister meant there was one more person to boss Emma around.

Right now, Katie just wanted to be back in her own neat, quiet house, with no one but Pepper to play with.

But that wasn't going to be possible. At least, not until the magic wind returned to turn her back into Katie Carew. And who knew when that was going to happen? She took the sponge from the sink and began to wipe up some of the tomato sauce. It was the least she could do.

As she cleaned, Katie's stomach grumbled slightly. She was getting hungry. The Weber family would probably be hungry soon too. Unfortunately, they wouldn't be having much of a dinner tonight.

Just then, Katie felt a cool breeze blowing on the back of her neck. She turned to see if Mrs. Weber had come back to the house. But the front door was shut tight. She shifted her head slightly to look at the kitchen window. It was closed too.

Katie knew what that meant.

Within seconds, the magic wind was blowing at full force, swirling harder than ever. The wind circled around Katie, faster and faster, practically lifting her off the ground.

Then it stopped. Just like that.

Katie stood up slowly. She opened her eyes and peered at her reflection in the oven's glass door. Gone were Emma's long, straight, brown braids and big, brown eyes. Katie's own red hair, green eyes, and freckles were all back in place.

Katie had changed back into herself. But nothing in the kitchen had changed. It was still a disaster. And Mrs. Weber would surely be home soon!

Chapter 12

"Oh, no. What a mess," Emma said as she wandered into the kitchen. She looked kind of dazed.

"One of the twins spilled the tomato sauce," Katie explained.

"I know," Emma began. She shook her head slightly, trying to figure out what had just happened. "I kind of remember something about Timmy knocking over the sauce. But I'm not really sure. It's like I was there, but I wasn't." She groaned and put her hand to her forehead. "Oh, I don't even know what I mean."

Katie sighed. She understood *exactly* what Emma meant.

"I'd better finish cleaning up before my mom sees this," Emma said, picking up a sponge. "I can't believe Timmy did that. Where are the twins, anyway?"

"I think they're trying to hide from bath time," Katie told her.

"They're going to be cranky soon," Emma thought out loud, looking at the clock over the stove. "If they don't eat dinner on time, they get horrible."

Get horrible? Katie thought. _How much worse could they be?_

"I guess I'd better call my mom on her cell phone and tell her to get more sauce for dinner. I hope she hasn't left the supermarket already," Emma said as she headed for the phone.

Katie had a better idea. "Don't call her," she said.

"But she'll need the sauce to make dinner."

"How about _we_ make the dinner?" Katie suggested excitedly.

"I don't know how to cook anything," Emma said.

"I do," Katie said proudly. "I've learned lots of recipes in my cooking class."

"I'm not allowed to use the stove or the oven unless there's a grown-up around," Emma told her.

"Me neither," Katie said. "But we can make plenty of food without them. Like ants on a log."

"We're going to eat *ants*?" Emma asked.

"No. We're going to use raisins. They look like ants."

Emma laughed. "This sounds like something Mr. Guthrie would make us eat."

"It's delicious," Katie promised. "You'll see. You get the celery. I'll get the raisins and the peanut butter."

Katie showed Emma how to fill the inside of each of the celery stalks with creamy peanut butter. Then she placed four raisins on each stalk.

"Tada!" Katie exclaimed once she'd finished. "Perfect ants on a log!"

"That looks good," Emma said. "But it's not enough for a whole dinner."

"Well, what other ingredients do you have?" Katie asked.

Emma peeked into the refrigerator. "We've got lettuce, red peppers, tomatoes, carrots, tuna, bananas, and chocolate sauce. Oh, and we also have this package of raw meat my mom took out of the freezer."

"We can't serve raw meat," Katie reminded her.

"I don't think tuna and chocolate sauce sounds very good, either," Emma added. She wrinkled up her nose at the thought of it.

"No, but we could make a salad and put tuna in it."

"Oh, that sounds yummy," Emma agreed.

"And we could slice the bananas and pour chocolate sauce on them for dessert," Katie continued.

"Is that one of the recipes from your cooking class?" Emma asked.

Katie shook her head. "I made that one up myself," she said proudly.

Katie began to chop the vegetables and put them in a big glass bowl. Emma sliced the bananas and covered them with a thin drizzle of chocolate sauce. They finished just as Mrs. Weber came home.

Emma's mom stopped and stared at the kitchen in amazement. The table was set beautifully. There was an ants on a log appetizer at each place. The salad was in the middle of the table. "What's all this?" Mrs. Weber asked, surprised.

"Emma thought you would like it if someone else made dinner for you tonight," Katie told her.

Emma smiled gratefully at her. It had really been Katie's idea, after all. Katie winked back at her.

"Wow!" Mrs. Weber seemed really pleased. "Thank you, girls!"

Just then, Lacey came downstairs with the twins. Tyler still had tomato sauce on his hands and face. Timmy had clay in his hair. Katie had no idea where *that* could have come from.

"Mom, Emma didn't give the twins a bath," Lacey said. It was obvious she was angry about having to get off the phone to help when the tomato sauce spilled. She wanted to get Emma in trouble.

But that's not what happened.

"Your sister and her friend just made this lovely dinner for us," Mrs. Weber told Lacey. "You should thank them. And while I know I asked Emma to bathe the twins, it's actually *your* turn to help me with them. I shouldn't have to ask Emma to do your chores, Lacey."

Lacey scowled, but said nothing.

"Please take the boys upstairs and clean them up," Mrs. Weber continued. "And hurry. I don't want to keep this delicious dinner waiting."

Katie and Emma exchanged smiles. It was good to see Lacey get in trouble. Especially after the way she'd yelled at Katie. (Although Lacey had thought she was yelling at Emma.)

"I've got to go," Katie told her friend.

"Aren't you going to stay and have supper with us?" Mrs. Weber asked. "You and Emma worked so hard."

Katie thought about all the things Timmy and Tyler could do with tuna, peanut butter, celery, bananas, and chocolate sauce. It wasn't a very delicious image.

"No, thanks," Katie said as she walked toward the door. "My mom's probably already made my dinner."

"Good-bye, Katie, and thanks," Emma said.

"You're welcome," Katie told her. "I'll see you in school on Monday. That's our first day of band!"

Chapter 13

Hot cross buns. Hot cross buns. One a penny. Two a penny. Hot cross buns.

Katie struggled to play her first song on her clarinet. It was really hard getting the sound to come out of the instrument. She hoped it would be better once she started taking private music lessons. Her mother had hired a clarinet teacher who would come to the house on Saturday mornings. But her teacher couldn't start until next week.

Katie wasn't the only one having a difficult time making her instrument sound right. The band room was filled with beginning musicians, and everyone was struggling with their new instruments. They were all having a tough time of it.

Becky was trying to cover the holes on her French horn while blowing at the same time. She wasn't being very successful.

Emma W. had picked the flute as her instrument because it always sounded so pretty. But today, Emma's flute didn't sound very pretty. It just sounded squeaky.

Instead of getting her own saxophone, Miriam Chan's father had given her one of his old ones. Unfortunately, it was too big for Miriam. She had to stand to play it and blow very hard. Her whole face was beet red.

Kevin *looked* very professional holding his trumpet. It was obvious his brother Ian had shown him how to do that. Too bad Ian hadn't taught Kevin how to keep his spit *inside* the instrument. The way Kevin moved his lips to play the trumpet made him spray all over the place.

George's tuba was huge. It was also very

loud. George played louder than anyone else in the beginning band. Unfortunately, he couldn't play the notes at the same time as everyone else. His timing was completely off. And Kadeem . . .

"Whoops!" Kadeem shouted as his trombone slide slipped off its track and flew across the room.

Mr. Starkey jumped out of the way just in time to miss being hit by a flying trombone slide.

"Sorry," Kadeem said as he scrambled to pick up the slide.

Mr. Starkey smiled at him. He didn't say a word. He just stood in the front of the room moving his arms back and forth as the children played.

It didn't sound much like music to Katie— just a lot of squeaks and squawks with an occasional banging from Jeremy on the drums. She never would have recognized this as "Hot Cross Buns." But Mr. Starkey seemed to like the way the children had played it.

"That was very nice," the music teacher said at the end of class. "Pack up your instruments carefully. I'll see you all next Monday. Don't forget to practice."

As the kids packed up their instruments and got ready to go back to class, Mr. Starkey adjusted his tie, and slipped into his sport jacket. It seemed odd to see a teacher dressed so nicely after Katie had spent so much time in Mr. G's classroom. Mr. Starkey was nothing like Mr. G. The band director had short, neatly cut blond hair. His shirt was pressed, and he wore slacks instead of jeans. Mr. Starkey was a normal teacher. Except he taught music, of course.

"That was fun!" Emma said as she placed her silver flute in its case. "I can't wait to go home and practice." She sighed. "I'll just have to make sure the twins aren't taking a nap."

Becky Stern turned around and smiled at Jeremy. "Your drums sounded great," she told him. "You have really good timing."

Katie laughed. She knew Becky had a major crush on Jeremy.

Jeremy blushed. "Thanks," he said gruffly.

"This is harder than I thought it would be," Katie admitted. "I had trouble just getting my mouth to stay in the right shape around the reed."

"Me too," Kevin said. "I have to keep my lips buzzing all the time. All this drool comes out."

"We know," Katie, George, Becky, and Emma said at once.

Katie gently placed her clarinet in its case, and began to walk back toward class 4A. There was still a half an hour before it was time to go home. The kids who weren't taking band were still in the classroom having free reading time.

"Hey, Katie, wait up!" Jeremy called after her.

She stopped and turned around. "What's up?"

"The most exciting thing ever!" Jeremy exclaimed. "The coach said I can start in Sunday's game."

"That's so cool," Katie said sincerely. She knew how much he'd been looking forward to being a starting player.

"My mom said I could bring one friend to the game. Do you want to come and watch?"

Katie was so happy. It was nice to know that she and Jeremy were still best friends even though they were in different classes. "You bet!" she said excitedly. "I'll even bring the snacks. We learned how to make the most delicious sandwiches in last week's cooking class!"

"Awesome!" Jeremy replied. "We'll pick you up at around eight-thirty. Then after the game, my parents will probably take us for ice cream."

"Great!" Katie said excitedly. "It'll be just like the old days."

Chapter 14

"I jump high, I jump low. Touch my shoulder, touch my toe. Spin around, jump real high. I reach straight up and grab the sky!" Emma W. leaped up as she finished her jump-rope rhyme.

"That was great, Em," Jessica told her.

"Thanks," Emma said. "Now I'll take your end so you can jump."

"Okay," Jessica said. "Then, when I miss—and I always do—I'll take Katie's end."

It was recess time on Tuesday afternoon. Katie, Emma, and Jessica were all playing jump rope together. Emma and Jessica knew lots of rhymes Katie had never heard before.

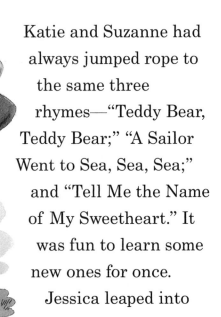

Katie and Suzanne had always jumped rope to the same three rhymes—"Teddy Bear, Teddy Bear;" "A Sailor Went to Sea, Sea, Sea;" and "Tell Me the Name of My Sweetheart." It was fun to learn some new ones for once.

Jessica leaped into the turning rope and began to jump. "I went to the store for something sweet, along the way, who did I meet . . ." she began. Within seconds, she tripped over the rope. "See, I told you. I stink at this," she groaned as she went over and took Katie's end of the rope.

"But you're a great ender," Emma assured her.

"That's because I get lots of practice," Jessica joked. "I'm always on the end." She began to turn the rope.

"Teddy bear, teddy bear, turn around," Katie sang as she jumped. "Teddy bear, teddy bear, touch the ground. Teddy bear . . ."

"Hey, there's Suzanne," Jessica called out. She waved to her. "Suzanne, you want to jump rope?"

Suzanne shook her head. "I was going to kick around a soccer ball," she called back. "Why don't you come over here and play with me? *Just the two of us.*"

Jessica looked at Emma. "Sorry, gotta go," she said, dropping the rope before Katie was finished jumping.

Katie and Emma stared as Jessica raced off.

"I don't believe Suzanne!" Katie shouted angrily. "That was really mean."

"Jessica's changed so much now that we're in fourth grade," Emma sighed sadly. "She used to be a lot of fun. She had the best ideas for things to do. Now all she does is follow Suzanne."

"Yeah," Katie agreed.

Emma turned to Katie. "So I guess you and Suzanne aren't best friends anymore, huh?"

Katie shrugged. She was mad at Suzanne, but she wasn't willing to give her up as a best friend. At least not yet. They'd been friends for a long time. Besides, Katie didn't think this was all Suzanne's fault. "Her mom wants her to play with the kids in her new class for a while, so she can get to know them. I guess that's what she's doing."

"But that's silly," Emma said. "You can have new friends and still play with your old ones. It's like this song my mom sings to Matthew and the twins. 'Make new friends, but keep the old. One is silver and the other's gold.' "

"That's a nice song," Katie told Emma. "It's kind of like you, Jeremy, and me. You're a new friend. He's an old friend."

"I don't know Jeremy very well," Emma said. "We haven't been in the same class in a while."

"Maybe one day we could all hang out at my house together," Katie suggested. "You could bring Matthew. I bet he'd love having a *big* boy to play with."

"Wouldn't Jeremy mind playing with a first-grader?" asked Emma.

Katie shook her head. Jeremy was an only child, just like her. He'd love having a little kid around . . . for a while, anyway. The best part about Matthew was that after you were done playing with him, he went home with Emma. "He'd like Matthew, I'm sure."

Emma smiled, a little. But she couldn't seem to keep her eyes from where Jessica and Suzanne were.

"Come on," Katie urged her new friend. "Let's go ask Mandy and Emma S. if they'll jump rope with us."

"Okay," Emma said slowly.

"It'll be fun," Katie assured her. "Class 4A girls rule!"

Chapter 15

When Katie got to school the following Monday, there was a big surprise waiting for class 4A. There was a large glass cage on the table in the back of her classroom. They had a class pet!

Or did they?

The thing inside the cage wasn't exactly a pet. At least not yet.

"It's an egg," Kevin announced to everyone.

"A *weird-looking* egg," George added.

George was right. Something about this egg looked different—but no one could quite explain why.

"What type of egg is it?" Emma S. asked Mr. G.

"You'll have to wait and see," Mr. Guthrie replied.

"I wonder what kind of bird's gonna hatch out of an egg like that," Kadeem muttered. "Probably a cuckoo bird."

"The cuckoo bird has been extinct for thousands of years," Mandy reminded him.

"No, it hasn't," Kadeem replied. "George is still here."

George turned red in the face. He opened his mouth to speak, but Mr. Guthrie placed a calming hand on his shoulder.

"Save it," Mr. G. told him. "We'll schedule a joke-off for this afternoon. You can get him then."

George nodded and smiled at Kadeem.

Katie might have been disappointed about her class pet being an egg, but she was still excited that it was Monday. Monday was band day. At her private clarinet lesson on Saturday, Katie's teacher had taught her two new songs! She couldn't wait to play them for Mr. Starkey.

But it turned out Mr. Starkey wasn't interested in new songs. He was still working on "Hot Cross Buns."

"Okay, everyone, instruments up," the band teacher said in his mild-mannered voice. "Begin."

Hot cross buns. Hot cross buns. One a penny. Two a penny. Hot cross buns.

The band sounded a little better than the week before. Strange noises were still coming from George's tuba, and it sometimes sounded like there was a mouse running around in Kevin's trumpet. But you could tell that the song was "Hot Cross Buns." At least Kadeem was able to keep the slide on his trombone this time.

"Okay, that was much better," Mr. Starkey assured them. "Let's try it again."

Katie raised her hand.

"Yes, Clarinet?" Mr. Starkey was calling

the kids by their instruments until he could memorize everyone's real name.

"Aren't we going to play any other songs today? I learned 'Go Tell Aunt Rhodie' and 'Merrily We Roll Along' at my private lesson this past Saturday."

"That's very nice," Mr. Starkey complimented her. "But we're working on 'Hot Cross Buns' as a band."

"But I . . ."

Mr. Starkey shook his head. "There's no 'I' in band," he replied calmly. "We work as a team. The team has to get *this* song right before it can move on."

Katie frowned. She was getting really sick of "Hot Cross Buns."

Suzanne was waiting for Katie on the playground after school. "You want to have a playdate?" she suggested. "Maybe we could go to your house and play jump rope or something."

"Sure!" Katie looked around. "Where's Jessica?"

"Dentist's appointment," Suzanne told her.

Katie frowned. "So I was your second choice?"

Suzanne shook her head hard. "I didn't want to play with her today. My mom said it was okay for me to play with my old friends now. I've missed you."

"Well, you haven't been acting that way," Katie told her.

Suzanne looked down, embarrassed. "I guess I've been kind of mean to you lately."

"More than *kind of*," Katie corrected her. "The only person you talk to is Jessica."

"Well, you and Emma W. are real close now, too, you know," Suzanne replied. She sounded jealous.

"But that doesn't mean I don't want to play with you too," Katie replied.

"I guess." Suzanne shook her head sadly. "Things have just been so weird for me this year. You and I aren't in the same class. There's so much more homework. The classwork is a lot harder. I've been kind of scared." She frowned. "But I guess it wasn't right of me to let it all out on you."

"*Everyone* has been nervous," Katie assured Suzanne.

"Not you. You made a new friend. You got used to your class right away. You seem happy."

"I'm happy *now*. But it took a few weeks for me to get comfortable. It would have been easier for me if you and I had played together at recess sometimes. Maybe it would have been easier for you too."

"I guess so. I acted pretty dumb. Will you still be my friend?" Suzanne asked nervously.

Katie smiled. "I never stopped," she assured her.

"Katie, you're the best. I sure wish you were in my class."

Katie smiled. She was glad Suzanne had said that. *Finally*.

"You'd like it in 4B. Ms. Sweet's just like her name," Suzanne told her. "She's not at all strict like Mrs. Derkman. Today she gave us candy chicks for snack. They were yummy."

"I'll bet," Katie agreed. "We had cheese and crackers."

"Well, that's nutritious, anyway," Suzanne said.

"The worms and mud were better," Katie told her.

Suzanne laughed. She'd heard all about that. "You guys do some weird things in there."

"I'll say," Katie agreed. "You should see the strange thing we got for a class pet."

"Ooh, we got our class pet today too," Suzanne said excitedly, not waiting to hear what Katie's class pet was. "She's the sweetest guinea pig. She's got fuzzy brown and white fur that sticks up all over the place. I wanted to call her Coco Chanel, but the class voted for Fluffy. It's an okay name, I guess."

"We got an egg," Katie replied. "We're going to watch it hatch."

"What's inside?"

"Mr. G. says it's a surprise."

"Oh." Suzanne shrugged. "Anyway, at free time we built a playground for Fluffy with blocks and let her run around in it. She had a good time climbing up and down on the stairs, and crossing over this amazing bridge that Manny built."

Katie didn't know what to say to that. Their class egg didn't do anything but lay there.

"So what are you going to wear to the all-school picnic this year?" Suzanne asked, changing the subject. "I think I'm going to wear my new dark green corduroy jeans and my white shirt with the sequin trim. Maybe we can go together. Like last year."

Katie had almost forgotten about the all-school picnic. It was the one afternoon when the elementary school kids and their families could get together with the teachers and not think about school.

"Sure. We can go together. But I haven't thought about what I'm going to wear yet," Katie admitted. "I've been too busy with homework, cooking class, and band."

"How's band?" Suzanne asked her.

"It's kind of dull. Mr. Starkey does the same song over and over again."

"I thought you really wanted to play the clarinet."

"Oh, I like the clarinet. I just don't like band," Katie explained. "Mr. Starkey is sooooo boring. He doesn't let us try anything new. He just stands there in the front of the room waving his arms up and down. He's not even like a real teacher. He's got the easiest job in the whole school."

Suzanne glanced over Katie's shoulder. A funny look came over her face. "Uh, Katie," she whispered quietly.

"What?"

"Don't turn around."

Of course, that made Katie turn around real fast.

Oh, no! Mr. Starkey was standing behind her. Not close behind her, but probably near enough to hear what Katie had been saying. Katie had been talking pretty loud.

The teacher had a frown on his face. But he didn't yell at Katie. In fact, all he said was, "Have a good week, Clarinet. Don't forget to practice."

As Mr. Starkey walked away, Katie scowled. "I HATE MONDAYS!" she moaned.

Chapter 16

Katie may have hated Mondays, but she couldn't stop them from coming. Before she knew it, it was time for another boring beginning band rehearsal. YUCK!

Katie walked into the band room and put her music book on the stand. Then she placed a fresh reed in her clarinet.

Katie looked around to see who else was in class. She saw Becky and Jeremy walk into the room.

"It was so cute the way you made that little soccer ball for Fluffy," Becky said to Jeremy. "I loved watching her push it around her cage with her nose."

"She'd make a great offensive player," Jeremy agreed. "On a guinea pig team, anyway."

Katie sighed. The kids in 4B were having such a good time with their class pet. The egg in Katie's classroom didn't look any closer to hatching than it had the week before.

"Hey, Katie, you want to come over and hang out after school today? My drum lesson isn't until six o'clock. That gives us plenty of time to play," Jeremy asked.

Katie opened her mouth to answer, but shut it just as Mr. Starkey entered the room. Katie figured her music teacher was probably upset enough with her because of what she'd said last week. Katie didn't want to make him any madder by talking during class.

Mr. Starkey opened his briefcase and frowned. He shook his head slightly, opened his desk drawer, and looked inside. "I think I left my conductor's baton in the teachers' lounge," he told the class. "Clarinet, will you go get it? I believe it's on the counter next to the coffee machine."

Katie nodded. She put down her clarinet and walked out of the class. As she left the room, she heard Mr. Starkey say, "Okay, everybody. Open your books to 'Hot Cross Buns.' "

✕ ✕ ✕

Katie knocked gently on the door to the teachers' lounge. There was no answer. All the teachers were in their classrooms, teaching. She opened the door and walked inside.

Katie had never been in the teachers' lounge before. It was nothing like she'd expected. It looked sort of like a living room. There was a big cloth couch, as well as a few comfortable chairs set around a big wooden table.

The coffeemaker was near the back of the room. Sure enough, Mr. Starkey's black-and-white conducting baton was sitting beside it. Katie reached for the baton.

But before she could lay a hand on it, a powerful wind began to blow all around Katie. This time, it hadn't started as a cool breeze, or a gentle draft, but she knew exactly what kind of wind it was.

The magic wind!

The powerful tornado swirled wildly around Katie, whipping her red hair in her eyes, and lifting her skirt high in the air. Katie was really glad she'd worn shorts under her skirt for gym class today.

The wind was so intense, Katie was sure it was going to blow her away. Far away. Like to another country or something. She shut her eyes tight and tried not to cry.

And then it stopped. Just like that. The magic wind was gone.

And so was Katie.

Chapter 17

Slowly, Katie opened her eyes. She stood up and looked around. She was in the school hallway, just outside the band room. The magic wind hadn't blown her very far, after all.

But who was she? Her hands were large and hairy, with blisters on the insides of her palms. Yuck!

Her shoes were definitely men's brown loafers. She was also wearing a men's button-down shirt and slacks. Okay, so she was a man. But *which* man?

Nervously, Katie looked at her reflection in the window in the band room door. A familiar face peered back at her. The face had blue eyes, neatly cropped blond hair, and a small hole in the right ear. Katie had turned into Mr. Starkey! And Mr. Starkey had a pierced ear. How wild was that?

Ugh. Earring or no earring, she'd still turned into her music teacher. Now she'd have to hear "Hot Cross Buns" for the rest of the school day.

Or would she?

Katie was Mr. Starkey now. She could ask the band to play any song she wanted. Katie smiled excitedly as she walked back into the band room.

✕   ✕   ✕

"Okay, everyone, turn to page eight," Katie told the beginning band. "We're going to play 'Yankee Doodle.'"

The kids all turned the pages in their books. Katie raised her hands in the air and got ready to conduct the band.

"Mr. Starkey," Miriam interrupted. "What's this weird symbol doing next to this note?"

"That's a B-flat," Katie told him. "My teacher taught me about flats and . . ."

"Your *what*?" Kadeem asked.

Oops. Katie *was* a teacher now. She'd almost forgotten. "I mean, didn't your saxophone teacher show you that?"

Miriam shook her head. "We're not up to page eight yet. I'm still working on 'Go Tell Aunt Rhodie.' How do you play a B-flat on a sax?"

"Can you show me how to play it on my flute too?" Emma W. asked him. "I had to skip my lesson last week because of a doctor's appointment."

Katie frowned. She had no idea how to play a B-flat on a saxophone, flute, or any of the other beginning band instruments, except for the clarinet.

Then she remembered that from time to time Mr. Starkey kept a lot of music books and papers in his desk. Maybe there was something in one of them.

Katie opened the top desk drawer. There was a pile of papers inside. She rustled through them, looking for a chart or a picture—anything that might show her how to make a B-flat on a sax or a flute. But there was nothing like that in the drawer.

Instead, Katie found herself looking through a pile of poems with names like "Fire in My Brain," "Love Strikes Like Lightning," and "I Can't Take No More." They sounded like rock song titles or something.

Whatever they were, they weren't going to help Katie right now. She dug deeper into the drawer. "Oops," she mumbled as a pile of photographs fell to the floor.

She bent over and picked up the pictures. "Whoa!" she exclaimed.

"What?" George asked, practically leaping out of his tuba.

"Yeah, what?" Kadeem echoed.

"It's Mr. Starkey . . . I mean *me* . . . playing drums in a rock band. Wow. How cool is that?"

She studied the photo. There was Mr. Starkey in a tie-dyed shirt and a bandana sitting behind a huge drum set. The name of his band—the Downhill Slide—was written across the bass drum.

Becky looked at her curiously. "Didn't you know you played in a rock band?" she asked, confused.

"I . . . er . . . of course I did," Katie stammered. "I just didn't know I had the pictures here. Anyway, let's get started with 'Yankee Doodle.' If there's a note you don't know, just skip it, and go on to the next one."

"Won't that sound weird?" Jeremy asked her.

Katie shrugged. "I don't think so."

"But . . ." Kevin began.

Katie looked at the kids. "Come on, you guys. You don't want to be playing 'Hot Cross Buns' for the rest of your lives, do you?"

Chapter 18

Katie raised her arms and began to conduct just the same way Mr. Starkey always did. But it didn't seem to be working. The kids weren't following her rhythm at all.

To make it worse, her arms were starting to hurt. Conducting the beginning band was hard work!

OOOOOOMMMMMPAAAA! George's tuba sounded like it was going to explode.

Squeeeeeeeeek! Emma's flute sounded like chalk scratching against a blackboard.

Kevin blew so hard into his trumpet that spit flew everywhere.

"Ooh, gross!" Becky shouted. *Clang!* She

dropped her horn as she reached to check the
back of her head for spit.

Jeremy kept drumming, trying to keep
up with the different rhythms Katie was
conducting. He was throwing everyone else
completely off.

"Stop!" Katie shouted finally. "Put down your instruments."

The kids all looked at her strangely. Mr. Starkey had never made them stop before the end of the song before. And he'd never yelled at them. When Mr. Starkey wanted the kids to put their instruments down, he simply lowered his arms.

"That was awful," Katie told the kids. "You sound like you've never played before."

"We've never played *this* before," Kevin reminded her. "I've never even seen some of these notes."

"Me neither. I skipped all the ones I didn't know. I finished before everyone else did." George sounded really proud, like he'd won a race or something.

Katie frowned. "You guys can play this correctly if you want to. *I* learned it."

"Of course you did. You're a music teacher," Kadeem reminded her.

Oh, yeah. Katie had forgotten again.

"You're right," she told Kadeem. "And it's my job to teach you this song. So let's try it again."

Katie raised her arms. The kids picked up their instruments and started to play.

Yikes! The song sounded even worse this time. It seemed like whenever someone didn't know how to play a note, they just played the wrong one louder.

In the middle of everything, Katie heard a loud bell ringing. It didn't sound like any instrument she knew.

"Mr. Starkey," Jeremy shouted loudly over the noise. "The classroom phone is ringing."

"What?" Katie screamed.

"The phone!" Jeremy yelled even louder.

"Okay, everyone, keep working on the song," Katie shouted as she picked up the phone and took it out into the hall.

"Mr. Starkey!" the voice on the other end shouted.

"Who is this?"

"Mr. Kane!"

Katie gulped. It was the principal. He sounded really mad!

"What is going on in that classroom?" Mr. Kane demanded.

"We're practicing," Katie told him.

"Well, stop it. I've been getting complaints from teachers all over the school! There are still classes going on, you know!"

"But it's a new song and . . ."

"That's not a song!" Mr. Kane insisted. "It's noise. Why can't you get those children to play correctly?"

"You're not being fair!" Katie told him. "I'm trying. It's really hard being a music teacher."

"If you can't control your students, I will. I'm coming to the band room right now."

Katie dropped the phone. Oh, no! The principal was coming. She was going to be in big trouble.

Right then, Katie didn't care that she was

supposed to be a grown man. She was a fourth-grade girl who didn't want to get in trouble with the principal. So she did what any scared fourth-grade girl would do. She ran into the girls room to hide.

As she opened the door, two girls began to scream, "There's a man in the girls bathroom!"

Oops! Katie had forgotten she was Mr. Starkey. Quickly, she raced out into the hall-way, and looked for a place where she could be alone.

The teachers' lounge. There was no one in there! She raced down the hall.

Katie hurried into the lounge and slammed the door shut. She hid behind the couch—just in case Mr. Kane tried to look for her in there. She was way down the hall from the band room, but she could still hear the kids practicing, just like she'd told them to. They sounded awful! No wonder all the teachers had been complaining.

Then she heard loud, angry footsteps

coming down the hall. That had to be Mr. Kane. What a mess the magic wind had gotten her into this time.

Just then, Katie felt a cool breeze on the back of her neck. She knew what that meant.

The magic wind had returned!

The wind picked up speed. Before long, a full-power tornado was swirling rapidly around Katie. She closed her eyes tight as the magic wind turned faster and faster. It spun her around like a top.

And then it stopped. Just like that.

Katie Kazoo was back.

But where was Mr. Starkey?

Katie heard a loud noise coming from the band room.

Oh, no! Mr. Starkey was in trouble.

Big trouble!

Chapter 19

Katie raced out of the teachers' lounge and darted down the hall. She reached the band room just moments after Mr. Kane did. She could hear the principal speaking angrily to Mr. Starkey.

"What a racket!" he shouted. "Haven't you been able to teach these children anything?"

"They know 'Hot Cross Buns,' " Mr. Starkey told him nervously. "We've been working very hard on it."

"That didn't sound at all like 'Hot Cross Buns' to me," Mr. Kane insisted.

"That's because we were playing 'Yankee Doodle,' " Kadeem interrupted. "It's a hard song. Most of us haven't learned all the notes yet."

"Then why were they playing it?" Mr. Kane asked Mr. Starkey.

"They weren't," he replied.

"Yes, we were," Kadeem insisted.

"Well, I mean, they were, but they shouldn't have been. They must have . . . oh, I don't know. It's all so fuzzy." The music teacher sounded very confused.

"Mr. Starkey, you and I will discuss this later," Mr. Kane said angrily. "As for you, children, everyone in this band must add an extra sixty minutes of instrument practice a day to his or her homework."

George gasped. "That's an extra hour . . ."

"A day!" Kevin finished his thought.

"Yes. Every day. Without fail. That's what you'll have to do if you want to stay in the band," Mr. Kane told them.

George slipped out of his tuba. "Then I'm out of here!"

"Me too," Kevin agreed. He took his trumpet and walked out of the band room.

"Hey, you guys, wait for me!" Kadeem added, running after them.

"I don't have time for an hour a day of practicing—not with soccer and everything," Jeremy told Mr. Starkey as he handed him his drumsticks.

"Jeremy, wait for me," Becky called, running after him.

Emma W. couldn't handle the new rule, either. "I'm sorry, Mr. Starkey," she said sweetly as she left the room. "I have a lot of chores at home. It was hard enough for me to fit in fifteen minutes a day."

Mr. Kane looked around the empty band room. "Well, that's that," he told the music teacher. "You'll have to focus your attention on the fifth and sixth-grade performing groups. I hope you have better luck with them. I was hoping to have a musical group perform at the all-school picnic this year."

The principal stormed out of the room. Mr. Starkey was left alone, wondering what had happened.

Chapter 20

That afternoon, Katie went to Jeremy's house to play. George, Becky, and Kevin came along too.

"Wow, Katie, you really missed it," Jeremy told her. "Mr. Kane was so mad."

"Imagine him wanting us to practice an hour a day. Fifteen minutes was plenty," George added.

"The band's lousy, anyway," Kevin added. "Mr. Starkey's a crummy conductor."

Katie frowned. Everything that had happened in band today had been her fault— not Mr. Starkey's. Of course, she couldn't tell her friends that.

"Mr. Starkey's just plain chicken," George continued. "He let Mr. Kane yell at us when it was all his fault."

"He acted like he didn't even know why we were playing 'Yankee Doodle,'" Becky agreed.

"I'm glad I'm out of the band," Jeremy said. "Music's for geeks like Mr. Starkey."

"Now that I don't have to practice my French horn, I can spend more time on my gymnastics," Becky agreed. She did a perfect cartwheel. "Gymnastics isn't for geeks."

Now Katie felt really bad. Not only had the kids all quit the band, but now they hated music too. This was awful!

"We sounded so horrible," Jeremy continued. "It hurt my ears. *AROOOOO!*" He howled like a dog in pain.

Becky laughed and howled too. "Hey, maybe we can do a howling duet at the all-school picnic," she joked.

George covered his ears. "Maybe *not*," he told her.

"The all-school picnic! That's it!" Katie shouted out suddenly. She leaped up and began to run back toward Cherrydale Elementary School.

"Where are you going?" Jeremy called after her.

But Katie didn't answer. She didn't have time. She had to save the fourth-grade beginning band!

Mr. Starkey was in the band room putting away some sheet music when Katie arrived at the door. He looked up at her and sighed.

"Are you giving up the clarinet too?" he asked.

Katie shook her head. "No way. Music's fun."

"You're the only fourth-grader who seems to think so." Mr. Starkey shook his head. "I can't believe the kids don't love playing their instruments. Music is the greatest thing there is. And musicians are really cool people."

"But none of us have ever met a real musician," Katie replied.

"*I'm* a musician," Mr. Starkey reminded her.

"Yeah, but we think of you as a teacher. The kids at school have never seen you drum with the Downhill Slide."

"How did you know about my band?"

Katie gulped. "I . . . um . . . er . . . I just heard about it," she said quickly. "Anyway, I bet the kids would think music was awesome if they could see you in a tie-dyed shirt, drumming with a rock and roll band. You could even wear an earring."

"How did you know I used to wear an earring?"

Katie sighed. Mr. Starkey was missing the point. "I just think if you and your band were to play at the picnic, the kids would see how cool music could be. Then maybe . . ."

"Maybe they'd join the beginning band again," Mr. Starkey finished her thought. He shrugged. "It's worth a try, I guess."

"Then you'll do it?" Katie asked excitedly.

"Sure. Why not? The guys and I always love playing for a live audience. Even if your plan doesn't work, we'll have a fun afternoon."

"Oh, it will work," Katie assured him. "It just has to."

Chapter 21

"Katie, I can't believe you won't try this fried chicken," Suzanne said between bites of her drumstick at the all-school picnic. "It's unbelievable."

"You know I don't eat anything that ever had a face," Katie reminded her.

"Come on, Katie. One bite," Suzanne waved the drumstick in the air.

Mr. Guthrie was walking by while the girls were talking. He turned and smiled at Katie. "Don't let her tease you, Katie Kazoo," he said. "I'm a vegetarian too. Have you tried the corn on the cob?"

Katie smiled. It might have sounded funny

if a different teacher had called her Katie Kazoo. But Katie was getting used to the fact that Mr. G. was no ordinary teacher.

"You vegetarians don't know what you're missing," Suzanne told them both. She took another huge bite of chicken and looked up at the stage. Drums, microphones, and electric guitars were all set up there. "I wonder who this mystery band is."

Katie smiled. For once, she knew something before Suzanne did. "You'll find out soon," she told her. "The sign said they'd be going on at two-thirty. It's almost that time now."

Sure enough, a few moments later, Mr. Kane took to the stage. "Is everyone having fun?" he shouted into a microphone.

"YEAH!" the crowd of kids, teachers, and parents all shouted back to him.

"That's great!" the principal cheered. "Now get ready to dance. Please welcome the Downhill Slide, featuring our own Mr. Starkey on drums!"

Mr. Starkey and his band ran onto the stage and began playing one of their rock songs.

All the kids rushed to the chairs and sat down in front of the stage.

"Check out Mr. Starkey!" Emma said to Katie. "I can't believe that's really him!"

Katie smiled.

Just then, Jessica pushed her way toward them.

"Hey, make some space for me!" Jessica shouted over the music.

"You can slide right in here, Jess," Emma said.

Katie smiled again. It looked like Jessica and Emma had made up, just like she and Suzanne had.

"Check out Mr. Starkey!" Suzanne exclaimed. "He's dressed like a rock star."

It was true. The music teacher was wearing a tie-dyed tank top and a pair of jeans. He had a purple bandana tied around his head.

"I think he's wearing an earring," Miriam

gasped. "Look. There's a hoop in his right ear."

"He's a really good drummer," Jeremy added. "Check out the way he's banging those cymbals."

"I think he must practice a lot. You can't get good at an instrument unless you do," Katie remarked.

Kevin and his brother Ian bopped over to where the fourth-graders were standing.

"You guys are so lucky," Ian told the fourth-graders. "Your music teacher's cool. When I went to Cherrydale Elementary, the music teacher was a real geek. He'd never play awesome music like this."

The kids all looked at one another.

"He *is* kind of cool," Kadeem had to admit as Mr. Starkey jammed on his drums. "It's like having a rock star right at our school."

"I wonder if *I'll* ever be that good on drums," Jeremy wondered out loud.

"You won't be now that you quit playing," Katie said.

"Who says I quit?"

"You did," Katie reminded him.

"Yeah, well . . . I un-quit!" Jeremy declared. "I think being a musician is awesome."

"Me too," George agreed. "You guys think I could play rock-and-roll tuba?"

Katie giggled.

At the end of the song, the audience cheered wildly. Mr. Starkey grinned and spoke into his microphone. "Thanks, Cherrydale!" he exclaimed. "The next song we're going to play is kind of new for us. But we've been practicing it a lot this week. We're dedicating this tune to a very special member of the beginning band! This song goes out to you, Clarinet."

The kids all stared at Katie. She smiled back at them.

"One, two, three," Mr. Starkey shouted out as he tapped his sticks in the air. The band started to play.

"I know this song from somewhere," Becky said.

"It's really familiar," Emma agreed.

"I don't think they play it on the radio," Suzanne said.

"So where have we heard it?" Kevin wondered.

Katie listened to a few more notes. "Oh my gosh!" She started to laugh. "That's 'Hot Cross Buns' . . . with a rock beat!" she declared.

Chapter 22

Katie was really psyched to go to school on Monday morning. She couldn't wait to get to band practice, so she could work on "Hot Cross Buns." Maybe Mr. Starkey would let the kids turn it into a rock song, just like the Downhill Slide had.

But band practice wasn't the only exciting thing happening in Cherrydale Elementary School. As it turned out, life in class 4A was pretty thrilling too.

When the kids walked into the classroom on Monday morning, they found Mr. Guthrie standing by the glass tank. "Yo, dudes!" the teacher greeted them. "Come here. The egg is starting to hatch. Look at how cool!"

Katie threw down her bookbag and ran toward the back of the room. She peered into the tank. Sure enough, their class egg was finally cracking.

"Our baby bird is coming!" Mandy shouted excitedly.

"This is amazing," Andrew added. "I've never seen a bird hatch before."

"Me neither," Kadeem said.

"Do you think it will be able to fly right away?" Emma S. asked Mr. Guthrie.

The teacher shook his head. "I think that's out of the question."

"But what if it wants to spread its wings and fly?" Katie asked. "It wouldn't be fair not to let it. Animals have rights too."

"I agree," Mr. Guthrie said. "But in this case . . ."

"Flying isn't going to be something *this* pet will want to do, Katie Kazoo," George interrupted. He pointed into the cage.

"Whoa!" Kadeem shouted. "It's not a bird. It's a snake!"

Sure enough, a baby snake had emerged from the egg. It was red with black, white, and yellow markings.

"Is it poisonous?" Emma W. asked Mr. Guthrie. She nervously moved away from the cage.

"It's harmless," he assured her.

"I didn't know snakes came from eggs," Emma S. said with amazement.

"Sure," Mandy told her. "Snakes are reptiles, just like turtles and lizards. All reptiles hatch from eggs."

"That's right," Mr. Guthrie agreed. "We're going to learn a lot more about reptiles in the next few weeks. That's our new science unit."

Kevin looked over at the beanbag chairs in the middle of the room. "No more birds, huh?"

Mr. Guthrie shook his head.

"Oh, well. There go our nests!" Kevin said. "What should we call our new pet?"

Andrew asked.

Katie watched the snake slither out of its egg. It was cute the way he slinked around the bottom of his glass cage. "How about Slinky?" she suggested.

"That's a great name," George told her.

"I like it too," Kadeem agreed.

"Hey, George and Kadeem finally agree on something," Andrew pointed out.

"Now we *have* to name the snake Slinky," Mandy told the class.

Mr. G. grinned. "Slinky it is."

The way Katie saw things, the kids in 4A were really lucky to have Mr. Guthrie for a fourth-grade teacher. A normal teacher would never have brought a snake egg to school. But what was so great about being normal? Forget about guinea pigs and hamsters. No animal in the whole school was cooler than Slinky!

Take that, class 4B!